One Day
A Stranger Came

Story by Naomi Wakan
Art by Tatjana Krizmanic Volz

Annick Press
Toronto • New York

Once upon a time there were three friends, John, Ivan and Giovanni. Their farms all butted up to each other like this.

Their lands had been worked by their families for many generations. Each farm had a farmhouse, a barn and a chicken run, but they all shared the

water, which came down from the mountains in a winding brook. They also shared a duck pond. "How could they share a duck pond?" you will ask. Well, if you think about it, sharing things isn't that difficult.

"Spring is here," the children would shout, when the snow had melted and the soil had warmed up, and John, Ivan and Giovanni ploughed their fields. Their wives, Sally, Helen and Rosi, sowed the vegetable and herb gardens near their farm houses. When the planting was done, all the families sat down to a big party and everyone wished for a good year's harvest.

As Spring turned to Summer, the children weeded the fields. When the corn was ready, everyone helped harvest it. When Fall came around, the families harvested potatoes and later carrots and onions, so that by winter everyone had a good store of food. They all joined in preparing corn roasts, preserving, and, best of all, Thanksgiving dinner. In fact, any event on the farms turned into a party since the families enjoyed being together so much.

In winter the snow was too deep for the children to go to school, so they went to each farm in turn. At John's and Sally's the children learned to make baskets and hats using rushes from the edge of the duck pond. Helen taught them how to spin and weave using wool from the family's sheep. And Rosi showed the children how to make pottery using clay from the banks of the brook that flowed into the pond.

"Times are good," said the friends, "how fortunate we are!" But when bad luck did come around, such as when Rosi's and Giovanni's youngest child lay in bed very pale and silent for many days, that was when the families helped each other a lot.

One day in early Spring, when the men were having lunch down by the duck pond, an important-looking stranger rode up on a horse. He handed each of them a notice, and he announced that Berland, Monland and Talland had decided to make their boundaries very clear in order to stop the fighting

between their countries. John and Ivan and Giovanni looked bewildered. "What fighting?" they wondered. They had been friends for so long that they had completely forgotten that each of their farms was in a different country.

"That means," said the stranger, in a serious and solemn voice, "that because you each live in a different country, you must look at this map and build fences to mark the boundaries."

John, Ivan and Giovanni scratched their heads and were very upset.

"But how can we divide the brook that we share?" they all said together. "That's for you to figure out," the stranger said in a severe voice. Then he turned his horse and galloped off.

John, Ivan and Giovanni called their families together to announce the bad news. Everyone cried.

"Let's just not do it," said the children, but their parents were worried. Eventually Rosi spoke up and said as cheerfully as she could, "We've stood together through good times and bad times and this is not going to part us. We have to make fences, but we can put gates in, can't we? That way we can visit as usual."

They helped each other make the fences and everyone built big gates in each fence. Sally, with her beautiful handwriting, painted "Welcome" on each sign. Then she hung a sign over each family's gate. Now they still visited and helped one another, although maybe just a bit less than before.

Later that year, the stranger returned to inspect the fences. He was fairly satisfied with what the families had done, but he had some new rules to announce.

"Each of your countries has its own form of education," he began pompously. "Since the children live so far from the schools, and they cannot attend during the winter, each family will be sent lessons, and because each country has its own lessons, the children must study separately."

"This will make things more difficult for the children," said John to the stranger. "When they learn together they help each other out..."

"That idea is of no consequence to the authorities," said the stranger, unmoved. "These are the rules and you had better follow them." And before anyone could move, he was gone.

"Let's study together anyway," said the children. But the parents were too worried to let them.

That winter was certainly different from others. Susan and Tom studied in their own home, as did Dimitri and Sonya, and Guido and Alberto. Soon the children were playing on their own, too. Having to go through gates seemed to make everything different. For the first time that anyone could remember,

the families' Christmas party was not so joyous. Everyone tried hard to have a good time, but they remembered the fences dividing their farms, and things just weren't the same.

In Spring, when the snow started to melt, the stranger came to discuss the watering of the fields. "Since the brook runs through Ivan's property," the stranger declared, "John and Giovanni will have to pay money to him for using his water..." Ivan shook his fist in protest, but the stranger continued, "and Ivan will have to pay some of the money to his government." The families could hardly believe their ears when they heard the news, and Ivan felt very ashamed when his old friends came to pay him. For while there was always plenty of food on the farms, money was scarce.

That year the families didn't plant their crops together, nor did they weed together. They were all terribly upset that things had got to such a sad state. But they were also angry with themselves and each other because no one had done anything earlier. John and Sally said cross words to Ivan and Helen, and Ivan shouted at Giovanni and Rosi, who in turn called angrily across the fence to John and Sally.

How could old friends fight like this?

They were standing outside one afternoon, arguing, when suddenly Sonya appeared. She climbed up into the apple tree.

"Stop it," she called to everyone. "Stop fighting like that."

The families were very surprised, and they quieted down and listened to her.

"Don't you remember," she began, "don't you remember the great corn roasts we used to have? And when we all used to jump in the duck pond to cool off? And we had the best parties... and I had lots of friends? Now no one plays with anyone else because the man from the government told us to put up these fences and not be friends. I hate it being like this and I want it to stop now!"

She stomped very hard on the branch and slipped. Everyone rushed forward to catch her.

Helen, her mother, took her in her arms and called out, "Neighbours, we have work to do, and there's no time to lose!"

They all followed Helen into the house and sat down around the large kitchen table, just like in the old days, and Ivan began:

"Well, Sonya is right for sure, because none of us like the fences that separate us... and you all know how I feel about the money I have to take from you for the water..."

"Yes, yes," everyone nodded.

"The fences we can put up with, but you paying me for the water just doesn't feel right. It comes down from the mountain as a gift to all of us. Sometimes I wish we could stop it up there..."

"How about making it into a fountain right at the bottom of the cliffs?" shouted Tom. "Then the water would splash and dribble all over the place and not just run through Ivan's land!" He threw his arms around, pretending to be a fountain.

"Well, how about that!" cried John, his face breaking into a smile.

The parents started to laugh, just in little embarrassed chuckles at first. It seemed as though it had been a long time since they had laughed together. Soon, the chuckles became giggles and hoots and they began to slap each other happily on the shoulders.

When silence finally settled, Rosi asked thoughtfully, "Would a fountain really work... ?"

"Well, now, it sounds a little wild," said Giovanni, "but who knows? Tom might have something there. Best thing is that we'll be working together again. That way we'll come up with an answer for sure. Tell you what though, we'd all think better with some food in front of us."

Everybody smiled and nodded in agreement.

Ivan sat down in the corner and started to write a letter to the authorities explaining that because the families wouldn't be using the brook as a source of water any more, they wouldn't be paying any money in future.

Meanwhile everyone else began to help prepare a meal. They all felt like singing as they worked together and the children skipped and danced as they set the big table.

Then the three families sat down to eat,
happy that they were friends once

more, and they promised each other never
to let fences come between them again.

Annick Press gratefully acknowledges the support of the Canada
Council and the Ontario Arts Council.

Canadian Cataloguing in Publication Data
Wakan, Naomi.
  One day a stranger came

ISBN 1-55037-354-4 (bound). – 1-55037-353-6 (pbk.)

I. Volz, Tatjana K. (Tatjana Krizmanic).   II. Title

Ps8595.A3305 1994   jC813'54   C93-094548-4
PZ7.W35On 1994

The art in this book was rendered in pastels.
The text was typeset in Garamond by Attic Typesetting.

Distributed in Canada by:
Firefly Books Ltd.
250 Sparks Ave.
Willowdale, ON M2H 2S4

Published in the USA by Annick Press (U.S.) Ltd.
Distributed in the U.S.A. by:
Firefly Books Ltd.
P.O. Box 1325
Ellicott Station
Buffalo, NY 14205

∞ Printed on acid-free paper.

Printed and bound in Canada by
D.W. Friesen & Sons, Altona, Manitoba.